WITHDRAWN

Save that Sunflower!

First published in 2010
by Wayland

Text copyright © Andy Blackford
Illustration copyright © Richard Watson

Wayland
338 Euston Road
London NW1 3BH

Wayland Australia
Level 17/207 Kent Street
Sydney, NSW 2000

Series Editor: Louise John
Cover design: Paul Cherrill
Design: D.R.ink
Consultant: Shirley Bickler

A CIP catalogue record for this book is available from the British Library.

ISBN 9780750262149

Printed in China

Wayland is a division of Hachette Children's Books,
an Hachette UK Company

www.hachette.co.uk

Save that Sunflower!

Written by Andy Blackford
Illustrated by Richard Watson

WAYLAND

It was spring and Ruby was helping Dad in the garden. She planted lots of sunflower seeds.

Merlin wanted to help.
He liked digging.

When Ruby went inside for
a drink, Merlin dug up all
the seeds!

"Oh, Merlin!" said Ruby.
"What a mess!"

So Ruby planted some more seeds. She watered them every day.

"We are going to have lots of sunflower plants," she told Merlin.

The sunflowers were soon tall and yellow.

But the sun was hot and there was no rain for days and days.

"I think your sunflowers are thirsty," said Dad.

"Let's water them with the hose," said Ruby.

"No!" said Dad. "When there
is no rain, we must all help
to save water."

Then Ruby had a good idea. After her bath, she used some pots and pans to collect the water.

Then she poured the water onto the sunflowers.

"Good idea!" said Dad.
"That's called recycling!"

Next day it rained and
rained. Ruby and Merlin did
a rain dance in the garden.

Ruby and Merlin were covered in mud! Dad washed it off with some rainwater.

"Oh, that's cold!" said Ruby.

"Woof!" said Merlin.

"Maybe this recycled water will make you two grow just like the sunflowers!" laughed Dad.

START READING is a series of highly enjoyable books for beginner readers. **The books have been carefully graded to match the Book Bands widely used in schools.** This enables readers to be sure they choose books that match their own reading ability.

Look out for the Band colour on the book in our Start Reading logo.

The Bands are:

Pink Band 1A & 1B

Red Band 2

Yellow Band 3

Blue Band 4

Green Band 5

Orange Band 6

Turquoise Band 7

Purple Band 8

Gold Band 9

START READING books can be read independently or shared with an adult. They promote the enjoyment of reading through satisfying stories supported by fun illustrations.

Andy Blackford used to play guitar in a rock band. Besides books, he writes about running and scuba diving. He has run across the Sahara Desert and dived with tiger sharks. He lives in the country with his wife and daughter, a friendly collie dog and a grumpy cat.

Richard Watson was born in 1980 and from as soon as he was able to read and write, he always had his nose in a book and a pen in his hand. After school, Richard went on to study illustration in Lincoln and graduated in 2003. He has worked as an illustrator ever since.